# MORGY MAKES HIS MOVE

# MORGY MAKES HIS MOVE

## by Maggie Lewis
### Illustrated by Michael Chesworth

Houghton Mifflin Company
Boston

# to Roswell, Sam and Eli, who gave me my start

Text copyright © 1999 by Maggie Lewis
Illustrations copyright © 1999 by Michael Chesworth
All rights reserved. For information about permission to repro-
duce selections from this book, write to Permissions,
Houghton Mifflin Company, 215 Park Avenue South, New York,
New York 10003.
www.houghtonmifflinbooks.com

The text of this book is set in 12.5-point Cheltenham.
*Library of Congress Cataloging-in-Publication data*
Lewis, Maggie.
Morgy makes his move / Maggie Lewis.
p. cm.
Summary: When third-grader Morgy MacDougal-MacDuff moves
from California to Massachusetts with his parents, he has a lot
of new things to get used to before he feels comfortable.

RNF ISBN 0-395-92284-4   PAP ISBN 0-618-19680-3
[1. Moving, Household—Fiction. 2. Schools—Fiction. 3.
Massachusetts—Fiction. 4. Family Life—Fiction.] I. Title.
PZ7.L58726Mo   1999
[Fic]—dc21
98-43245 CIP AC
Printed in the United States of America
MV 10 9 8

# CONTENTS

# ONE
# Morgy Makes His Move

The first day in my new school, the teacher said, "This is Morgy MacDougal-MacDuff." Everyone laughed.

There's no playground here. At recess, they throw dead leaves at each other. At my old school in California, we had a real boat for a sandbox, and you could see the ocean from the top of the slide.

Kids even laughed at my lunch. It was in a shiny pink shopping bag with sparkly plastic handles because Mom hadn't unpacked the little brown bags yet.

But Byron, who had black jeans, black high-tops, and black hair that stuck up straight in some places, sat right next to me in the cafeteria and didn't even smile. He said, "Want to go to the spa after school?"

I said I would. I didn't know what a spa was, but I didn't want him to laugh at me, too.

School got out early for teacher conferences. I would have been glad, but I knew my mother wasn't coming till 3:00. I stood on the steps. Kids rushed by. I didn't know where Byron was. Maybe I could go home on my own. I thought our house was big and yellow with an old tree in front, but I couldn't see it from where I stood. I started down the steps as if I knew where I was going so that no one would notice and laugh.

I looked up and down the street. All I saw was black claw trees and old houses that weren't mine. In California, the leaves are always green and they stay on the trees instead of clogging up around your feet when you try to go anywhere. The only thing I recognized from that morning was the crossing guard, with his sheep-dog mustache.

I wondered where my house was, why we had to move here, and why my parents gave me both their last names. "Cross!" barked the guard, so I did, but then I wondered what to do next. Kids were starting to stare at me.

Then Byron was standing next to me. "Come on," he said.

I didn't say, "Oh, no, I have to stand here for an

hour and a half and wait for my mom." I went.

It turns out a spa is just a little store. At least that's what it is in Puckett Corner, Massachusetts. We went to Mack's Spa and got chocolate milk. Mack pretended to try and pound our hands when we put our money down, so we kept whipping them away to get him to do it again. We drank our milk in there, sniffing the smell of newspapers and candy bars, till Byron had to go.

I stood looking out the door of the spa. I still had about an hour to wait for Mom, so I thought I'd go back to the school. But I couldn't remember the way we'd come. The houses on this street were all tall. They kind of leaned out over you. Windows stuck out from the roofs with their own pointy little roofs like surprised eyebrows. I didn't know which way to go. I was in trouble.

"Hey, sport, lose something?" asked Mack. Do you ever almost cry when someone is nice to you? I told him I had to go back to school or find a big yellow house with an old tree in front. I got a lump in my throat, but then in came a tall girl with long black hair that swung out when she jerked open the door. She needed toilet paper, fast. Her seven brothers and sisters and cousins had thrown all the toilet paper out the window at their grandmother's house. Her grandmother was really mad, and their mother wouldn't be home till late.

That sounded terrible. You could be lonely even with all those other kids around if your grandmother was mad.

Mack got her the toilet paper and put a little chocolate sampler in the bag. "For Grandma," he said. He asked her if she knew where there was a big yellow house with an old tree in front. She looked at me and said, "Not on my grandma's street. Call your mom," and left.

"I have no listing under those names," said the operator.

In came a lady with a blue knit hat. She said there were mysterious dark footprints way up in her third-floor bathtub, where no one ever went. That sounded scary. It would be hard to go into one of those tall old houses by yourself, even without footprints.

But Mack said the lady's nephew probably left those tracks when he painted the ceiling. He sold her some scouring powder and asked her about a big yellow house with an old tree.

"Now, there was one around the corner, but they painted it brown years ago," she said, and out she went.

I looked up the street. What if my house was

brown? Maybe Mom would come in on an errand and find me. But in came the crossing guard. He wanted Devil Dogs, but he was on a diet, so he guessed he'd just have some skim milk instead.

That sounded bad. I hate being hungry after school.

But Mack said a little popsicle wouldn't hurt. He sold him an orange one and asked him about a big yellow house with an old tree. The crossing guard said, "That kid's lost. Call the police," and left, licking his popsicle.

What if I had to go home in a squad car? I gulped down the rest of my chocolate milk, hard. In came Byron again, with a little girl and a big kid wearing a baseball cap.

The girl said there was a crying kitten stuck in a tree. She thought it was a stray. The big kid asked for cat food in a pop-top can. They could leave it at the bottom of the tree, and the kitten would jump down to get the food.

That sounded wrong. Kittens don't jump down from trees. I know, because I have one. They get out on a limb, and they don't know whether to go up or down, so they panic. You have to save them. I waited for Mack to say something, but he was getting the cat food. I guess he didn't know much about kittens.

So I said, "I can get kittens to come down. I know a trick."

5

"Do it!" said the big kid. They all ran out the door, and I ran after them.

We went up a hill and around a corner. There was a tall pine tree with mewing coming out of it. The big kid boosted me up, and I climbed all the way to where the kitten was. It was on the other side of a clump of pine needles, going "Mew! Mew!" I put my leg over the branch and leaned way out. I reached my hand out even farther and did my trick. I clicked my nails. It made a tiny sound, but the kitten heard it. It looked around in my direction, pointing its ears toward my hand.

It was orange and fluffy, just like my kitten.

It was my kitten. "Pancake!" I said.

"Meeew!" said Pancake. He slowly turned around. He got past the pine needles and came down the branch to me, paw over paw. He kept stopping and going "Mew?" so I had to click again, but that was OK. I was used to that. He did that in California, too. Finally he got close enough. I put my hands around his belly and gently pulled his little claws out of the bark. He started purring like a motorboat.

"Yay!" said Byron and the big kid. The little girl held her hands up as if she expected to catch us.

We were way up. I could see the school—right

around the corner, it turned out—and a big park. Eight kids were playing there while an old lady sat on a bench near them and ate a small box of chocolates. I saw the crossing guard help the lady with the blue knit hat across the street. She marched up the steps of a big, fancy house. I saw a church spire and cars quietly going around a square. From up this high, it all looked as neat and happy as a town in a train set.

Then I saw my mom. She was right next door, in front of a big yellow house with an old tree in front. "Pancake, here, kitty, kitty, kitty," she called.

"He's right here, Mom," I yelled down.

She jumped. "Morgy! I was just going to pick you up."

"We got out early, so I found my own way home," I said.

Then I climbed down, and we all went over to my house. Mom found us a box of cookies. The other kids turned out to be Byron's sister, Polly, and his brother, Tom. We made a fort out of empty boxes and played till it was dark and they had to go.

"Come again," said Mom, "now that you know where we live."

Now that *I* know where we live, I thought, but I didn't say anything.

# TWO
# Facing Ferguson

*Dear Keith,*

*How are you? I miss you. I don't know what anyone is saying around here. OK. They call a store a spa. Even this new friend I have, Byron. He has a mar. What is that? It's boring at recess, too.*

*Write soon,*
*Morgy*

I missed Keith most at recess.

Everyone else loved recess. There was a hill, a tree, and a sidewalk. You could run around on the hill or you could play hopscotch on the sidewalk. Some kids would go behind the tree and wrestle, but then Mrs. Caitland made them sit on the steps.

If you wanted to just stand around, you had to lean against the wall. Fifth-graders were waiting to stuff leaves down your back.

Byron and about six guys threw old tennis balls at the wall behind the gym and caught them. If you missed the ball, someone else could catch it and play. A couple of times, kids missed balls, but I didn't go get them. I thought maybe you had to be in the game already.

One day Byron threw the ball so hard it bounced all the way over to me. I jumped for it. It bounced off my shoulder and everyone laughed. So I just watched. A plane went over halfway through recess every day. It glittered like a little metal star. I thought it was going to California. I pretended I was on it.

"You don't want them to think you have a chip on your shoulder," Dad said. It was late. He had just gotten home from work, and he still had cold air around him from walking up our hill from his bus stop. He was sitting on my bed before I went to sleep. I thought he meant something wrong with my shoulder from the ball hitting it. But he said a "chip on your shoulder" meant deciding not to play the game without even trying it.

The next day, I crouched down like a catcher to show I would give it a try. Then I thought, they'll just laugh. Also, I might get leaves down my back. So I stood near the wall instead, with my knees bent. That way, I could jump out for the ball or lean back against the wall, fast.

The plane went over. I wondered if it was going to San Francisco or L.A. and what Keith was doing at his recess.

Someone yelled, "Heads up!" The ball hit me on the head.

It bounced straight up off my head, with everyone laughing. It went way up. But then I reached out and there it was, right in my hand. I looked at it a minute. Then I jumped out and threw it at the wall. It came back to me.

*Whop!* went my arm as I whipped it down. *Pop!* went the ball against the wall. This was great. *Whop, pop,* went the other kids, throwing. A kid caught my ball. I got it back. *Whop, pop.*

"Morgy!" Byron yelled.

I turned around, and there was a fifth-grader with his hands full of leaves. The bell rang. He grabbed the back of my jacket and stuffed leaves into it.

Then he lined up with his class as if nothing had happened.

I stood there with my mouth open. I was breathless. My neck was scraped. I was rustling.

"Ferguson!" yelled Byron as the fifth-graders marched quietly in. "Just because they're in fifth grade, they think they can do anything," he said. He pushed my hood inside out and leaves exploded from it. I shook out my jacket. We were late going in.

"Boys," said Mrs. Caitland, "you need to get in line when the bell rings."

I didn't say anything. I couldn't believe anyone would do that.

"A kid stuffed leaves down his back," said Byron.

"Who was it?" she asked. She looked ready to take on Ferguson herself.

"I don't know," said Byron. He shook his head at me.

"If it happens again, Morgy, call me and I'll come back there," said Mrs. Caitland. "Table monitors, please get out the humpback whale maps."

"If you tell that it's Ferguson," Byron said on the way to Mack's that afternoon, "he'll never stop doing it. I know because Tom knows his brother."

When I told Mom, she wanted to go right over and see the principal. I said Mrs. Caitland could handle it. I thought it would be even worse if Mom told on Ferguson.

"Wait till he does it again before you worry about it," said Dad that night, but I could tell he was worrying about it right then. "You just keep playing ball," he said when he turned out my light.

I just leaned on the wall the next day. But the day after that I found an orange and green tennis ball in the gutter on the way to school.

Play it!" said Byron when I showed him.

This time, everyone yelled *"AAAAHH!"* when they saw Ferguson coming. I froze. Then, *SCRUNCH, SCRUNCH, SCRUNCH,* the bell rang, and I was full of leaves.

"Don't tell Mrs. Caitland," said Byron, as we walked past a whole line of laughing fifth-graders.

The third time it happened, I told Dad.

"Well," said Dad, "don't get in a fight with him. Tell Mrs. Caitland."

"Byron says not to."

"Then you'll just have to face up to this Ferguson. Look him in the eye and tell him to stop," said Dad. I'd rather tell Mrs. Caitland, I thought.

The next time, I knew he was coming, but I didn't turn around. *SCRUNCH, SCRUNCH, SCRUNCH.* I didn't tell Mrs. Caitland, either. Ferguson knew I was scared of him, I thought. He would never stop. Being scared was making me more scared.

That afternoon, Mack's radio said it was going to snow. "Snow before Thanksgiving," he said. "Going to be some winter."

When I got home, Mom was knitting a mitten. Pancake was under the table with the ball of wool in his front paws. He was kicking it with his back paws. "Murl," he said, with his mouth full of wool. At least he was having fun.

In math the next day, I looked out the window. I could see a little drizzle of white. Clouds were wrapping up the sun like thick gray wool. Mrs. Caitland looked out, too, and said, "Well, let's try going out. Line up, everyone."

"Yay!" said everyone except me.

"This might be our last game, guys," said Byron. I saw Ferguson's green plaid coat and black tractor cap. At first the snow melted when it landed. It only stuck to the frozen mud puddles. Then the flakes got bigger. The tennis balls got wet and cold. They went *whop, plap, whop, plap.*

Then *"AAAAAHH!"* yelled everyone. I turned around and faced Ferguson.

I tried to look him in the eye. I said, "Don't," in a hooty, scared whisper.

He didn't look me in the eye. He just reached around behind me and stuffed in the leaves. They didn't scrunch. They were wet leaves, and cold. The bell rang. I kept looking at his face, but he turned around to go get in line. I grabbed his arm. He kept going. I held on. My feet slid on the snow. He walked with his head down, not looking at me but dragging me.

I was shaking. I was in line with him and the fifth-graders now. I was scared, but I couldn't let go of him. I also felt stupid. "Ferguson, look at me," I said in the same hooty voice, like a mad grandmother. Everyone laughed. I wished Dad had told me what to do next.

Then Mr. Johnson, the fifth-grade teacher, came down the stairs. He said, "Gentlemen." I let go of Ferguson. "Do you want to be suspended?" he asked.

"No," I said. Ferguson didn't say anything. He wouldn't look at me or Mr. Johnson. It got really quiet. The fifth-graders were staring. You could

hear snowflakes landing. My class went in. This is what it feels like to be the bad kid, I thought. I wondered if this happened to Ferguson a lot.

"Let's go visit the principal, shall we?" said Mr. Johnson. Ferguson shrugged. I wished I had never listened to Dad. Just then I heard the *clop, clop, clop* of high heels on asphalt.

"Morgy, come with me," said Mrs. Caitland. She grabbed my coat off me and shook it hard. Wet dead leaves flew everywhere. I followed her inside. *Clop, clop, clop.* She was mad. But we didn't go to the principal's office. We went back to our classroom.

"I don't know why Mr. Johnson can't control his class," she said when we got to the lockers. "Dear, I'm afraid we'll have to call your mother and get her to bring dry clothes."

"Don't call his mar. I've got a sweatshirt in my locker," said Byron. He was waiting in the hall.

"His mar," I said to myself. A mar was a mom.

"All right," said Mrs. Caitland. "I'll take your coat and put it by the radiator. Come in, boys, and we'll watch the whale video till lunchtime. Honestly, what a morning."

When my head came through Byron's sweatshirt, I saw he was laughing. "You should have seen

Ferguson! He didn't know what to do with you," he said. "They were laughing at *him*."

Mrs. Caitland came back out with my mitten. "I'm afraid you lost one," she said. "And it looks hand-knit, too."

I told her Mom was working on the other one. It kind of looked like a humpback whale. It was a little crooked. The tip was square instead of round, and the thumb was extra long. Byron said, "It'll be wam, though."

"Wam," I said to myself. I put on the mitten. My hand still stung from the cold, but the mitten was soft around it. I stopped shivering. I knew what "wam" meant.

# THREE
# Aunt Savanna & the Turkey Blizzard

*Hey Morgy,*

*Mar? What is mar? You only used to live on Vista del Mar. It's "ocean" in Spanish. Everyone misses you. Raul is feeding the lizard. Soccer is over. I'm bored, too.*

*Write soon,*
*Your buddy, Keith*

*whump!* A package landed on our porch. The Fed Ex truck zoomed away in a hurry. A blizzard was coming.

"More books for me to review," said Mom, but it was a pair of snow pants. Not normal snow pants. Red overalls with a blue kangaroo pocket on the front and yellow stripes down the legs. I could hear people laughing already.

But Mom was happy. "I knew I should put a rush on those," she said. "I guess I'm getting winter figured out. Look. Here's your other mitten, all finished, and the big storm is still down in the Carolinas." Dad and Mom were breaking their "no TV at breakfast" rule to watch a white blob eating a map of the East Coast. The mitten looked like another whale, going the other way.

"I called the airport," said Mom. "Your Aunt Savanna's plane is still scheduled to land at two, so I'll go get her. You're going home with Byron today."

I loved Byron's house. It was warm and full of stuff to play with, and it always smelled like gravy. When I told him my aunt was coming from L.A., he laughed. He called his Aunt Mary "ont," and I called my Aunt Savanna "ant."

It was the day before Thanksgiving. "Do you children want a snack?" called Aunt Mary when Tom, Polly, Byron, and I came in the front door.

"We stopped at Mack's," Byron yelled.

"I saw you, dear," said Aunt Mary. "But come up if you get hungry. Candy bars don't stick by you like cheese and crackers." Aunt Mary had a fuzzy green armchair with rockers that sat in the left surprised-eyebrow window in the top of Byron's house. She watched over the whole town, especially Polly, Tom, and Byron.

We lay on the rug in Tom and Byron's room and zoomed cars around. Tom snapped together the loop-de-loops in Byron's mini-auto-raceway for us. One car zoomed down the stairs and landed in Tom's boot. We tried to make it happen again. Just when we got one in my boot, Mom called to say Aunt Savanna was coming to pick me up.

It was time for Byron's hockey practice, too. We went up to Aunt Mary's room to get a hat she'd fixed for him.

"Wear the earflaps, dear, and don't make a face at Morgan," said Aunt Mary, just as Byron did. Up there, the ceilings slanted. You had to bend down to look out the window, but then you could see everything. The sky was gray and baggy like the ceiling of a blanket fort. The streetlights were on. Far away, on the turnpike, the headlights moved slowly, as if the darkness were extra thick that night.

"They had a traffic jam at noon," said Aunt Mary. "Everyone trying to get away before the storm. But where is it?" She looked out again. "This must be your aunt coming. She needs a hat."

Sure enough, my Aunt Savanna was coming up the walk fast, with her shoulders hunched up and her hands tucked in the bib of these weird red overalls she had on.

"Hey, those are my snow pants," I said.

"Oh, dear!" said Aunt Mary. She took my hand and pushed the cuff of my mitten down my coat sleeve. She frowned at the mitten. "Morgan, tell your mother she needs to decrease evenly. Then the mitten tips won't be lopsided like that."

Aunt Savanna buzzed.

The van full of guys going to hockey pulled up.

"Morgo!" said Savanna when I opened the door. She gave me one of her big, terrible hugs. She's nice and all, but her hair itches and she wears perfume that smells like jungle flowers with hot sauce. She's pretty strong, and she always holds on to me till I sneeze.

Over her shoulder, I saw Ferguson's green plaid coat in the van. "You're so big!" she said. "Look, your snow pants fit me!"

"Ah-choo!" I said.

"Bye, Morgy," said Byron as he got in the van.

"Your snow pants fit me!" said a shrill voice from the van, probably Ferguson's. "Look, MacDoof's got ladies' snow pants!" They all laughed. Byron ducked down to put his stick on the floor and waved silently to me.

They drove away, and we started to walk home. I thought of them in the van, laughing all the way to hockey, maybe all weekend. I didn't want to cry in front of Savanna.

"So, who's your friend?" said Savanna.

"Byron, I guess." I sniffled. "But he plays hockey and I don't."

"Pf!" said Savanna, making the noise she makes when you're being ridiculous. "I have friends who play polo." Savanna probably has friends on the moon. Mack waved at her when we passed the spa, and the crossing guard rushed out and made a bus and a dump truck stop so we could cross the street. He blew her a kiss as we went around the corner. "I stopped in for directions," she explained.

Mom was waiting for us in the front hall, with her coat on. "They had an opening, Savanna. I'll take the bus in case it snows," she said. "Sweetie," she said to me, "I have an appointment in Boston. I'll be back soon. Are you OK?" I smiled so she could go. Then I went upstairs to be alone.

My room is in the attic. I sat on the end of my bed and thought about my old room. I thought about soccer, and taco day in the cafeteria, and Keith. Big, fluffy flakes like moths started fluttering past the dead-looking maple tree outside my window. I cried.

Savanna came in and sat on my bed.

"Sorry I wore these. I was cold," she said.

"It's OK," I said. It wasn't, though. Those snow pants were trouble, especially now that Ferguson had seen Savanna wearing them. I would probably have to wear them to school on Monday, too. Sometimes you feel so bad you could almost hate your aunt.

"You know what?" said Savanna. "Those guys only make fun of you because they know it gets to you."

"How could it not get to me?" I said.

"I got called MacDoof in school, too, you know. Banana MacDoof."

"So what did you do?" I said.

"Cried. Then your grandma would say, 'If you want to make a friend, be a friend.' Grownups are always saying that, right?" Savanna forgets she's a grownup, probably because she's an art teacher. She finger-paints a lot.

"Well," she went on, "first I thought, pf! What am I supposed to do, pretend to be friends with these

26

mean kids? No thanks! Then I figured it out. You really have to *be* their friend. Think good things about them. Sometimes there was only one good thing. But it worked. I have all these friends now, and a lot of them used to call me Banana MacDoof."

"I think I'd rather just skip recess," I said.

"Oh, Morgo." Savanna tousled my hair and left. She had on furry purple slippers with googly eyes sewn on them. I could hear them whispering down both flights of stairs. Snow kept falling. I was all alone up there. Outside, the whole world went white.

Who wants to be friends with a MacDoof? I thought. Only Byron, and he's probably just being nice. Anyway, you couldn't be Ferguson's friend with all those leaves going down your back. Well, Savanna could. She wasn't afraid of anything or anyone. If she had had those snow pants, she would probably have worn them to school and laughed right back at the fifth-graders.

*"Dear Keith,"* I wrote. *"Help! I'm in a blizzard with Aunt Savanna."* Did mailmen go out in blizzards? I thought about putting it in a bottle and throwing it out the window. That reminded me of the Boston Tea Party. Mrs. Caitland wrote a play about it. We were supposed to practice our parts over the vacation.

I fell asleep trying to remember my lines and what Aunt Mary had said about mitten tips.

"Morgy," Savanna whispered. I woke up. It was darker inside and whiter outside. Dad had called. The storm was getting worse. He was going to stay in a hotel so he could spend Thanksgiving morning editing storm reports. Mom would join him, because the buses stopped running and she couldn't get home.

"We're orphans!" Savanna loves awful situations. Someone always rescues her and lets her wear his hat, like the captain of the Catalina Island ferry when she thought her cat went overboard. There are about a million Savanna stories. "Look, I found a hurricane lamp," she said. "Let's light it and have dinner."

We had toast-and-avocado sandwiches.

Savanna always makes me avocado sandwiches, ever since the first time Mom and Dad left me with her for the weekend. I was two or something. She took me to the beach. I got lost. Somehow, the lifeguard who brought me back found out it was her birthday, so all the lifeguards had a party for her. I went, too. The story goes that I ate a lot of avocado sandwiches for someone my size. They're especially good toasted.

"You've got four days till school," said Savanna. "Maybe they'll forget."

"They won't," I said, but I felt better. Maybe I was just hungry.

Then Mom called. "Sorry, Morgy," she said. "If we don't get home in time tomorrow, we'll have Thanksgiving on Friday. Don't let Savanna try to cook the turkey, OK? I love you."

We were sitting on the couch, along with some pieces of the stereo. Dad was going to put it together so we could listen to music with our Thanksgiving dinner. The only other thing in the living room so far was the TV, on a milk crate, and some dust tumbleweeds. Snow-light came in the tall, bare windows. On the news, a guy with his hair blowing stood in the snow. "They're calling this the Turkey Blizzard!" he yelled. "The question is, will it be worse than the blizzard of '78? Back to you, Chet and Nat."

I shivered. What if my parents never made it back? What if I really was an orphan? I thought of Byron getting home from hockey to his warm, crowded house. His aunt was allowed to cook.

A plow was grinding slowly up our street with a little snow in its shovel. In back, it sprayed sand and salt. I watched the snow come down some more. I made a promise, deep down inside, that if Mom and Dad got home, I would be a better friend to Byron. I would ask for hockey skates for Christmas. I would even be a friend to Ferguson.

Then the weirdest thing happened. The plow turned, snorted up our driveway, and stopped. There was a loud knock. Savanna opened the door. There stood a short man in a thick cap with snow on it. His coat collar was up around his ears. It was Byron's dad.

He looked up at the hurricane lamp Savanna was holding, and down at the googly-eyed slippers. He said, "Now, whose mar are you?"

"Mar?" Savanna said. "Excuse me?"

"Hi, Mr. Noonan," I said. "This is my aunt."

"Oh, there you are, Morgy," he said. "Thought I had the wrong house here for a minute. Byron's mar took another nurse's shift. Aunt Mary's at a garden club meeting—some kind of emergency about some begonias they're growing in the Town Hall basement. So Byron's mar is hoping the kids can stay with you people till Aunt Mary gets home. Just in case the lights go, you know."

"Hey, no problem," said Savanna. "Come on in, you guys. We'll make a fire and have s'mores!" So Tom, Polly, and Byron got out, and Byron's dad went plowing away, leaving us with a perfect, snowless driveway, just like in a Savanna story.

"So," said Savanna to Tom, "is it worse than the blizzard of '78?"

"It's not even a blizzard till it snows sideways," said Tom, "but Dad says people like to see the plows out before they go to bed. I'll get logs for the fire." He was acting more grown-up than usual. He looked happy. Maybe he was just secretly laughing at Savanna.

"Now it's a blizzard," he said when he came back in with the logs. He opened the chain curtains on our fireplace and clonked the logs in. He jammed newspapers underneath.

"Goody!" said Savanna, putting marshmallows on a barbecue fork. Outside, snow was going sideways—straight up in some places. It washed over the rooftops of the houses on our street like waves. It swirled like surf on their balconies and porches.

Savanna lit the fire. It smoked. Then it crackled. Then flames leaped up the chimney and went *whoom!*

"Ouch!" yelled Polly as Pancake jumped off her lap.

"Yikes!" yelled Savanna, and dialed 911.

# FOUR

## 911

The fire engine was there fast. A ladder went up. A fireman went up it. Another fireman ran in. "Everyone out?" he asked. We were all on the porch. Savanna held Polly. I held Pancake.

"Mroo," said Pancake, trying to jump out of my arms.

"You're from California," I said. "You don't want to jump in the snow." He settled down in my arms and panted, watching the light on the fire engine turn the snowflakes pink.

"Watch out below!" yelled the fireman. Something black sizzled into the snow. Then he came up on the porch. He took off his breathing mask and said, "Ma'am, that was a wasp's nest that caught fire.

You need to have the chimney cleaned every fall."

Polly climbed down from Savanna's arms and hugged him. He took off his fireproof glove and patted her hair, as if little girls always hugged him when he put out a fire. "There's no damage to the roof, which is a blessing," he continued. "I sprayed fire retardant down the chimney, but I think Franky got your furniture covered in there."

Polly said, "Are you bringing Franky to Thanksgiving?"

"Well, gee, Polly-Wolly-Doodle," he said, "we'll still be on duty. We'll come by later for a turkey sandwich."

Byron said, "This is our Uncle Mike. This is my friend Morgy and his Aunt Savanna. She's visiting from L.A."

Uncle Mike took off his hat and shook hands with Savanna. His hair stuck up. It almost touched the porch roof, he was so tall. The other fireman came out of the house. "There's some fire retardant on the hearth," he said. "Should mop right up, though." He got in the fire engine. Uncle Mike stayed on the porch.

"Sorry I couldn't offer you a s'more," said Savanna.

"You were making s'mores? Aw," he said. "I would have liked that."

Savanna was still smiling as she mopped up the black stuff on the hearth. Byron looked at me.

"She makes friends easily," I said.

"Yeah," said Byron, "Uncle Mike is just the same." Probably not, I thought, but Byron is so normal that he thinks everyone else is, too. That's why he's my friend.

We ate the s'mores ingredients. Now the TV reporter was out on a dark beach, yelling about a sea wall. Then they showed cars half buried in the snow on the turnpike. Polly lay on the couch. Her eyes kept closing. She was holding a piece of the stereo speaker.

"Why don't you all sleep over?" asked Savanna.

"Yes!" Byron and I said.

"I'll call Aunt Mary," Tom said.

There was no answer. Byron said Aunt Mary should be home by now. Tom said a tree might have fallen on the telephone wires.

"Maybe we should go see if she's OK," I suggested.

"Aunt Mary's OK," said Byron.

"She's probably just digging out our front walk," said Tom. "She likes to get an early start."

"Her snow boots have ice-grippers," said Byron.

"Mummy makes her leave them on the porch,

because they'll ruin the hall floor," said Polly, and she put her thumb in her mouth.

On TV we saw cars stuck under an underpass in Cambridge, people sleeping in a high school on Nantucket Island, and National Guardsmen getting ready to come to Boston with bulldozers. Polly was asleep. Savanna gently took the stereo piece out of her hand, put it on the floor, then covered her up. Pancake jumped up and sat in the crook of Polly's knees to take a cat bath.

Tom said he'd just sleep in Dad's desk chair in his coat, in case Mr. Noonan needed help plowing.

Byron gave me a "Yeah, right" look, and we went up to my room with some blankets. We put my window seat pillow on the floor for Byron's bed.

I went to the end of the attic and looked out the little round window under the point of our roof. You can see Aunt Mary's window from there. It was dark. Wouldn't she be watching on a night like this? I wondered. And shouldn't someone be watching over her? She's not even as tall as a snowdrift. But, I answered myself, if she needs help, it's probably not from some kid from California who's afraid of his own snow pants.

Then Byron was standing next to me. "You're worried," he said. "OK, we can go see her."

Savanna's door was closed. My snow pants hung on the knob. "She's had a long day," I said. So we didn't tell her we were going. Polly was snoring in the living room, and we could hear Tom playing a computer game in Dad's study.

Byron got on his plain navy blue snow pants. I put mine on. I had to. I tucked my mittens into my coat sleeves.

Outside, snowflakes swarmed into our faces. Snow was up to the window of Mack's Spa. It hissed and rattled through the bare tree branches. The road was white. It was bright and dark. The streetlights looked like melting marshmallows.

Going up the road to the Noonans' house was like wading in surf. I got sweaty. We staggered through a deep drift, and then our boots were rattling up the porch steps, which were blown bare by the wind. The door was locked. Byron rang the bell. On the porch were hockey sticks, snow shovels, two sleds, skates, a play pool, and a woodpile. Byron rang again.

"No boots with ice-grippers," I said. "She's not here."

"Maybe she's sleeping over in Town Hall," said Byron. "Except—wait." He looked at me. "My sled is missing."

"What would she do with your sled?"

"Save someone. I bet she went down to Main Street to save people stuck in cars."

We jumped off the porch, back into the drift. We rolled and waded back down the hill. As we crossed the intersection, a voice said, "Boys, does anyone know you're out in this weather?"

"No, Aunt Mary," we both said. A telephone truck was parked in the middle of the intersection, with a tent over the manhole cover. Byron looked into the tent.

"In here, dear," said Aunt Mary. She was sitting inside the truck.

"We were looking for you!" I said. "Are you OK?"

"You're helping the phone men?" said Byron.

She laughed. "I was coming over to check on you children. I saw the truck, so I reported that our telephone was out. They made me get in. They promised to drive me to your house, Morgan, but I think it's taking longer than they expected." She whispered the last thing. Then she said to the men in the tent, "I'll be going now! Thank you!"

"Lady," said a guy in a furry parka, "no one's supposed to be out unless it's emergency business," and he stood in Aunt Mary's way.

"This is an emergency," said Aunt Mary. "These are children!" She hopped right past him and we followed. She took the rope of Byron's sled. There was a shopping bag on it. "It's the turkey," she said. "Morgan, the stove in your house was gas when the Gradys lived there. I'm just hoping your mother didn't redo the kitchen."

"No," I said.

"Well, now, our electricity is also out, and I happen to know that Puckett Corner is always the last to get it back. I thought *only if* she still had the Gradys' nice big stove with the double oven, and *only if* she didn't need it all day, I might ask her to put our turkey in tomorrow. In the smaller oven, of course."

"We're not having a turkey till Friday, because Mom and Dad are in Boston and Aunt Savanna's not allowed to cook."

"We had a fire just making s'mores," said Byron. "Uncle Mike came, in a ladder truck."

"My," was all Aunt Mary said. She hopped into the plow tracks and set off for my house. The sled reared up. The turkey was surfing. We were panting when we got there.

Aunt Mary made us hang our snow pants on the

pantry doorknobs. She put the turkey in the refrigerator. Then she took off a tractor cap, her wool hat (with earflaps down), scarves, a gray wool coat, two pairs of mittens, and her ice-gripper boots. She found a plastic wastebasket and hung her clothes to drip into it. She got a stack of newspapers from the recycling bin and put her boots on it. She still had on gray wool pants under her dress. She looked in on Polly and Tom. Then she asked, "Do you boys want a cracker?"

We didn't. "Well, then, up to bed. I'll just beep your father." As I followed Byron up the back stairs, she reached out and tagged me. "Morgan," she said, "when you go out, especially at night and in a storm, you must tell the grownup in charge, however irresponsible. But that was very brave, dear, and I thank you."

# FIVE
# Blessings to Count

The next morning when we woke up, it was very quiet. Snow was flying past the windows like clothes in a dryer, and our house was full of a familiar gravy smell.

Aunt Mary was sitting in a chair next to the stove, looking at her watch. "Bring Morgan up to our house at two," she told Savanna. "We will not leave you to your own devices on Thanksgiving!"

"Let's have it here," said Savanna, who was making cinnamon toast. "This is supposed to be worse than the blizzard of '78!"

Aunt Mary thanked her kindly for the thought but said the Noonans had had Thanksgiving up at the top of that hill since before World War I, and that included the Great Depression, World War II, and the hurricane when Uncle Mike was born. She didn't think it mattered if this was better or worse than the blizzard of '78, and she basted the turkey.

Byron asked if Aunt Mary was going to pull the turkey back up the hill on his sled.

Aunt Mary said probably not, but once, during gas rationing, her mother did ride up the hill with a turkey tied to the handlebars of a bicycle.

That reminded Savanna of the time she invited some flight attendants over for Thanksgiving when their plane couldn't take off in the fog, because they had been so nice about lending her a raincoat when she went to London without her suitcase. They cooked the turkey in her apartment and took it out to the beach on a plant cart to share with the lifeguards. It fell off, but it didn't get too sandy.

"Oh, dear," said Aunt Mary, and looked out the round window by the front door. "Children, have you seen your father go by with the plow recently?"

No one had. Byron wanted to know if Savanna usually ate Thanksgiving dinner in her bathing suit.

"That time, I had to put on a sweatshirt," she said. "It's cold in the fog." Tom laughed and laughed.

She had my snow pants on again, too, with the googly-eyed, fuzzy purple slippers.

"I wouldn't impose on you," said Aunt Mary, looking past Savanna into the dining room, which looked like a garage when the cars are gone. Boxes and our folded-up dining room table were pushed up against the walls. It didn't look like a good place for Thanksgiving.

I didn't want the Noonans to hear any more Savanna stories, so I said, "Aunt Mary, have you been cooking the turkey ever since World War I?"

"Oh no, dear! During that war I made place cards," she said.

"I want to make place cards!" said Polly.

"So you shall," Aunt Mary said. "Perhaps Morgan has some old magazines. You cut out pictures of things to be grateful for, then glue them to cards. Byron and Morgan, you can write the names. Then we'll just see where we put them."

Savanna went in the dining room and started ripping tape off boxes. Tom went out to shovel snow. I found newspapers and catalogs. We didn't have any magazines yet.

"I need more pictures," said Polly. "I don't have enough things to be grateful for."

"What about this nice can of soup, right here?" asked Aunt Mary.

"It's tomato! Yuck!" said Polly.

"Sometimes it's hard work, counting your blessings," Aunt Mary said. She and Polly sighed.

Just then Mr. Noonan plowed up to the door, stopped his motor, and came in. "Still blowin'," was all he said. Savanna made him some toast, but he fell asleep before he finished it, in front of the TV, with the weatherman still talking. Aunt Mary leaned back in her chair by the oven and shut her eyes. Her ice-gripper boots stood by her feet. She wanted to go home, I just knew.

Then a person in blue, with a red plaid scarf flying out straight, came up the walk. "Mom!" said Byron. Polly ran outside. Mrs. Noonan came in with Polly gripping her leg, stomped off some snow, and said, "Is your mother back yet, Morgy?"

"No," I replied.

"She will be," said Byron's mom. She whispered to Aunt Mary.

Aunt Mary blinked and sat up. "Two! Well, bless her heart," she said. "Savanna, I do accept your kind invitation. We'll have Thanksgiving here. My, my!" She explored the back pantry. She got things out of the refrigerator. She made Byron's mom take a nap. She let Savanna baste the turkey. She opened a can of cranberry sauce.

The meal was ready at two. Probably the Noonans had been having it then since World War I. Just then the sun shone through a silvery hole in the clouds. Fluffs of snow drifted around outside, shining like tinsel. Inside, it smelled so good it made me dizzy.

"Now just look at that," said Aunt Mary. Savanna had put the dining room table together and unpacked the good china and silver. The Noonans' turkey sat in the middle, as if it belonged there. Savanna had found all the candlesticks. There were candles on the table and in the windows. There was even a big old six-candle one I'd never seen before, on top of a pile of boxes marked "Dining Room." The candles were red, green, white, and black. "I found them in a bag marked 'emergency' in the pantry," she said.

"Well, dear, that's what it is," said Aunt Mary, giving her a little hug. With that, the lights went off.

Mr. Noonan was saying grace: "...and, by the way, thank You for bringing us all together here, like Squanto and the Pilgrims, or something," when the door opened and in came Mom and Dad. Dad's glasses were fogged up. Mom was smiling.

Mom hugged me and looked all around. She got tears in her eyes. "Why, this is lovely!" she said, and sat down.

"Amen," said Mr. Noonan. "And may we have many more." Everyone began to eat and talk. Dad told how his friend from the newspaper gave them a ride partway home, then they walked a bit and along came a snowplow that brought them right to our door. Mr. Noonan said that must have been his friend Connor.

I told about the fire. Polly told how Uncle Mike put it out.

Tom told how the snow just filled in right after him when he shoveled. Mr. Noonan said the same thing happened to the plows, just like in '78. Aunt Mary told how Byron and I rescued her and the turkey, and here we all were.

Byron said, "I knew we should have dinner here."

"The best," said Tom, with his mouth full. Polly gave Pancake some stuffing.

"I did make a pie," said Mom. "I'll go get it."

"Oh, now, you just let us," said Aunt Mary. "That's your job now, letting people help you."

"Do you know what she's talking about?" Mom said to me.

"We thought you'd want to tell," said Byron's mom.

"I'm having twins," Mom said. "That's where I was—at the hospital, finding out. Byron's mother knew first, because she was on duty last night." Dad squeezed her hand.

I couldn't think of anything to say. I kept looking at Mom. She kept smiling. Savanna shook her head as if to say, "These grownups..." Polly said she'd babysit when she got old enough. Mr. Noonan proposed a toast.

Everyone said the pie was great, but I couldn't taste it. I kept thinking about the twins. I wondered where they would sleep, and if they'd call Mom "Mar." "And what if they're girls?" said Byron, thinking along with me. Then the grownups had coffee, and Aunt Mary told us how to wash the dishes.

When the lights went back on, we watched "The Turkey Blizzard Wrap-up" on TV. It was worse than the blizzard of '78 by two inches. Uncle Mike and Franky came for a sandwich, and then Franky took Polly, Byron, and Tom home in his new Jeep. Aunt Mary wrapped up the turkey and hugged Mom. She and Mr. and Mrs. Noonan went home in the plow. But Uncle Mike stayed to help Dad put the stereo together.

I went up to my room and finished my letter to Keith.

> *Dear Keith,*
>
> *Help! I'm in a blizzard with Aunt Savanna. Actually, it turned out OK. Actually, it was excellent. The chimney caught on fire. Byron stayed over. He got to ride in a snowplow. Was the blizzard on the news out there? I'll call you soon.*
>
> *Morgy*
>
> *P.S. Mom's having twins. Not right away, though.*

When I came downstairs to put it in the mail slot, I heard music. From the landing, I could see Uncle Mike and Savanna waltzing around the couch in our empty living room. Except it didn't really seem empty anymore, and probably never will.

# SIX
# Collision Zone

*Dear Morgy,*

*What did you get for Christmas? I got Collision Zone. It's on CD-ROM. Do you have that back there? Now school started again. We're doing a play. I'm Father Junípero Serra. When can you come visit?*

*Keith*

I did get hockey skates for Christmas. Dad took me to the rink. My ankles wobbled a little at first, but then I went faster. It felt cool. Dad said, what did I expect, after all that rollerblading?

So I signed up for hockey. The first time I went, I just watched. The kids skated fast, with their heads down. The coaches tweeted their whistles, and the kids stopped and pivoted around with their sticks down on that white ice just like the little guys in table hockey. I had a feeling I wasn't going to look like that.

The next Friday at practice time, Dad helped me put on everything but my skates. There was even special underwear, a jockstrap and a garter belt to hold up my socks. The socks went over my shin guards. Then padded pants with suspenders, shoulder pads, elbow pads, and a neck guard. I had to sit down. When practice started, I felt like a rack from a sports store sliding onto the ice with my stick.

That's when Ferguson noticed me. One minute he was at the far corner of the rink. The next minute I was looking down at his stick right near my skates. Then I was on my stomach, looking at the ice.

After practice, the coach said, "MacDougal, you're starting out fine. I'm not going to have you play on the team, though. Practice with us for the rest of the season. Then, if you're still interested, you can play next year." I was nodding. I didn't want to do anything too hard. Then Ferguson skated by and looked at me. I felt like a doof.

We had two practices a week. The Noonans and my parents took turns taking me and Byron. It had

been snowing since the Turkey Blizzard, so there were gray snow cliffs around the rink parking lot, and you had to go down this ice tunnel to get to the door. Byron and I sat together to put our skates on. We didn't talk. We had to listen to the coach. Well, Byron did, so that he could find out when the games were.

The beginning of practice is just skating around, hitting pucks. But mostly I tried to stay out of Ferguson's way. Whenever he got a chance, he'd skate by and knock me over. It wasn't hard to do.

Mom said, "I don't know if you should be around Ferguson with sticks, and those skate blades are sharp, too."

But Dad said there wasn't a part of me that wasn't covered with pads, which reminded Mom how much the equipment cost. "All right," she said, "but don't be a hero. Just skate away from him." Dad shook his head.

He talked to the coach. The coach made Ferguson sit in the penalty box, but he still tried to knock me over.

"Forget it," said Byron. "Ferguson is Ferguson." Sometimes he just looked at me, and I'd fall down. He didn't even laugh at me anymore. It was as if he didn't have to.

After practice on Fridays, we'd go change in the locker room and then get a slice of pizza. This was the good part. Byron's mom would pick us up and take us to my house. Byron's mom and Mom would get talking, and Byron and I would watch all these great Friday night TV shows and have cocoa.

Byron's mom was head of the Winter Fair at school, and Mom was doing the crafts table. She made little snowmen and skiers out of pompoms and knitted scarves in the school colors to spruce up used teddy bears. On Fridays, Mom and Byron's mom would have coffee, count the stuff, and make plans. They were raising money for swings for recess.

Probably even if I didn't want to go to the rink and get knocked over by Ferguson, I'd have to anyway, just to fit into the moms' Winter Fair schedule. But I would have felt worse being left home. Anyway, there was that promise I made at Thanksgiving when Savanna was here, about being a friend.

One night Mom and Byron's mom cut a huge snowflake out of a tarpaulin. On it they wrote

COME TO THE WINTER FAIR FEB. 28!
VOLUNTEERS NEEDED.

55

Byron, Tom, and I helped them put it up at school. It looked cool. The janitor said he'd take it down if it even looked like it would fall on the gym classes.

Byron's mom said, "I hope we get some volunteers."

But no one called. Every day when I got home, there were more snowmen, skiers, and scarves on the kitchen table. If one fell off, Pancake was ready. He'd shoot out from under the table and bat it into the laundry room. There were a lot of them in there. Mom said she wasn't bending over for just one snowman anymore.

"I'm worried," she said after dinner. "Laura Noonan is making signs, calling people, making all the cupcakes, building the snow maze, and who knows what else, all by herself."

"I'm sure Laura knows what she's doing," said Dad. "And you've got the babies to get ready for."

That Friday, Ferguson knocked me over, and I knocked over all the orange cones. Everyone laughed. Some kids fell on me just to join in. There were so many kids on top of me, it was dark. I decided to quit. But after practice, the coach tapped me on the shoulder. He skated over to the benches and I followed.

"MacDougal, it isn't your fault. But this is getting disruptive. You need some ice time, and I need to see some team-building. Here's what I'd like you to do: practice with the seven-and-unders. With a little more time, you'll stay up better. Next year you can play with us. Ferguson'll be long gone to the twelve-and-unders. I told their coach; he's expecting you." He waved at the guy at the other end of the rink and pointed at me. The other coach was Uncle Mike. He made a thumbs-up sign to me.

"Same practice time, just down there, OK?"

# SEVEN

# The Winter Fair

*Dear Keith,*

*OK. First I bring my lunch in a pink shopping bag and everyone notices. Then I get my own personal bully and doofy snow pants. Now I have to play hockey with first- and second-graders. How's the play going?*

*Morgy*

There was a kindergartner, too. The seven-and-unders were better skaters than me, but they fell down more than the ten-and-unders, so I fit in. And no one called me MacDoof. They thought I was some big kid named MacDougal, and Uncle Mike didn't tell them any different.

"So," said Mom one night at dinner, "the principal said the kids who have to stay in from recess for misbehaving can help Laura with the snow maze."

"Prison labor," said Dad.

"And..." Mom ignored him and served us more salad. "I thought I'd try teaching some of them to knit bear scarves."

"That would keep me on the straight and narrow," said Dad. I just hoped she didn't get mixed up with anyone I knew. No one had laughed at me for a while.

But even when I was practicing with the seven-and-unders, Ferguson managed to knock me over. If I was anywhere near the center line, there he'd be and down I'd go. Usually about three or four kids fell on top of me. The seven-and-unders were fast, but they couldn't stop very well. Uncle Mike gave us stopping drills.

"Skate fast to the blue line and stop, facing the stands. Then to the center line and stop, facing the same way, then back," he'd say, and he'd tweet his whistle. I used to like skating fast. But Ferguson was always at the center line when I got there. I'd slow down, then *wham!* I'd be in the dark, under a pile of kids. Uncle Mike said if I skated faster, there wouldn't be so many kids on top of me. I knew that. It's just hard to skate fast toward a catastrophe.

He showed me how to do a T-stop. You put one foot in front of you like a T. Then the other foot goes with it, your feet are sideways, and you stop. That is, if you don't crash into yourself and fall down. "Bend your knees and dig in," he said. "You'll get stronger, too. Don't worry."

Mom started going to school during recess. Some kid named Rudolf had plenty of time to learn to knit. "He has to stay in almost every day," she said as we ate our tuna noodle casserole one night. "At first he didn't look promising at all. But I sat him down in Mrs. Beeman's old rocker in the Guidance Office, and he's picking it right up. He comes in every morning and just turns out bear scarves. I think the rocking calms him down."

"I think Mom is getting more motherly," said Dad, patting her hand.

One night Ferguson knocked me down and I just lay there. I was tired. I looked up at the ceiling through the little puck-proof cage over my face, at these nets they have up there to keep pucks from hitting people in the stands. Like I would ever hit a puck. I was a puck. I had tears in my eyes and too much spit around my mouth guard.

Then there was Uncle Mike, looking down at me.

"You're fine, right?" he asked. I nodded.

"See, Morgy, that's what I was afraid of." He squatted next to me. "Ferguson is not the biggest or the best or even the ugliest player who will ever give you trouble. You've got to get right up, like we practiced. You can't lie down in a game, so handle it now. Get up, hustle, and dig in." He tweeted us into line. "Backwards to the blue line, turn around, forward to the center line, and stop," he said.

Skating backwards didn't fool Ferguson. When I turned around, there he was, watching me and planning his shot. I felt like I was in a race, but in slow motion. I could feel my cheeks jiggle when my skates hit the ice. I could hear my breath and the *chop, chop, chop* of the little kid skating right behind me, ready to fall on me. I saw white ice and the white faces of ten-and-unders turning toward me. I didn't want to fall down again. I had to do something.

So I tried "make a friend, be a friend." I bent my knees like the other kids. I ducked my head. Then I scrambled to think of a good thing about Ferguson. He's big? He's strong? He can skate?

"Dig in!" said Uncle Mike. Then I thought of it. He never says he didn't do it. I got up to the center line and did the T-stop. It worked. My skates went *kkkkkk.*

Ferguson's stick sort of bounced off them.

"Nice," said Uncle Mike. Ferguson looked surprised. I raised my glove to him and skated away. He gave me a little push. He was probably trying to push me over, but I guess he could have been patting me on the back.

That night the moms were excited. The principal said they could advertise the Winter Fair in the paper and let the public in. They could make more money. But the fair was in two weeks, and they didn't have enough crafts stuff to sell.

"All I have is two kindergarten mothers and you," said Byron's mom. "Maybe they have friends or mothers. What about that kid you were going to teach to knit?"

"Rudolf?" said Mom. "He's making progress. He doesn't go around looking guilty anymore. The other day he said hi to me. He doesn't even have to stay in so much anymore."

"Then he couldn't make a hundred more scarves," said Mrs. Noonan.

"Maybe he'd like a challenge," said Mom. "Maybe he'd stay in anyway."

"If this works," said Byron's mom, "we could have enough money for swings by spring."

"Then that Ferguson will have something to do

besides pick on third-graders," said Mom. Byron looked at me. I knew just what he was thinking about. Ferguson, swinging on a swing. "What are you boys laughing at?" said Mom.

Anyway, after I did the T-stop, Ferguson stopped hanging around the center line looking for me. I stopped feeling like the prey in a National Geographic special. Once I even got a puck in the goal during skating-around time. Uncle Mike said if I was seven or under, he'd play me.

A couple of nights after that, Dad sat on my bed and said, "Hey, I heard about that goal."

"It wasn't really a goal," I said.

"Well, Uncle Mike is pleased, Savanna says," said Dad.

"Savanna?" I said.

"Uncle Mike calls Savanna a lot," said Dad. "And of course Savanna calls Mom all the time. Great news, pal." He looked much happier. I knew he had been worried, but I thought it was about the twins.

Then it was the night before the fair. Byron and I sponged off bears, fluffed them with a hairdryer, tied their scarves, and packed them in our old moving boxes. Our kitchen was full of boxes with furry ears sticking out the top. Pancake got in a box with his ears sticking out, too.

"The bears, skiers, and snowmen can all go over in one load in our station wagon," said Mom to Byron's mom.

Byron made a bear say, "I get to sit in the way-back," in a squeaky voice, but the moms didn't laugh.

"Now, tomorrow," said Byron's mom to Mom, "I'll be out with the snow maze, and Big Tom will run the inner-tube raceway. You're in charge of everything inside the gym. We open at nine, so we'll set up at six-thirty."

We all got carpenter aprons with dollar bills in them for making change. Tom would sell cocoa. Byron and I were in charge of the "ice fishing" game. We had to help toddlers get prizes with magnets in a play pool.

The next morning Mom was all cheerful, even though it was really cold and the sun wasn't up yet. "Cherry blossom time where we come from, huh, puppy dog?" she said, and tightened the strings on my jacket hood. She was wearing a *Cat in the Hat* hat and Dad's orange jogging sweatsuit with her change apron tied under her sticking-out stomach. You could tell she was Savanna's sister. The Noonans' van stopped in our driveway and Mom jumped in. I rode with Dad and the bears.

In the gym Dad helped Mr. Noonan push tables

around. Byron and I stacked the bear boxes behind Mom's Cat-in-the-Hat Crafts booth. Then we sat in the play pool and had doughnuts.

"Hey!" said Byron. "What's Ferguson doing?"

In the shadowy corner behind Mom's booth, Ferguson was squatting down, picking up bears one by one, and looking around over his shoulder. "I'll get Dad," I whispered. But Mom was walking over there, so we ran to the booth.

"There you are, sweetie," said Mom. "Could you help Rudolf tie his last batch of scarves? He's been knitting and knitting, and I don't know what I'd do without him. Rudolf, this is my son, Morgy, and his friend Byron."

He was still crouching by the bears. He was making this horrible face, as if he'd been caught doing something bad instead of doing something good. He looked as if it were about the worst day of his life. Maybe it was, since Rudolf was also Ferguson.

"We've met," said Byron, picking up a bear.

"Thanks, guys," said Mom. "Now, where did I put those bean bags and penguins?" and she hustled away.

"Shut up, you guys," said Ferguson.

"We didn't say anything," said Byron. We didn't have to.

66

# EIGHT
# Swings by Spring

*Dear Morgy,*

*The play went OK, if you don't count my beard falling off every other minute. Soccer started. We travel! Raul is goalie. How's the hockey? Over? Take it easy, buddy.*

*Keith*

*P.S. Mom says to remind your mom about our double stroller.*

*Whop, pop, whop, pop.* Tennis balls were hitting the side of the gym one Saturday morning like popcorn popping. Clouds were zooming past. One moment our shadows would jump up on the bricks; the next moment they'd be gone. *Whop, pop, whop, pop,* jump,

jump, jump. There were five of us. Our parents were on the hill, putting up the swing set. *Whop, pop, whop, pop.* The snow was gone. It felt good to play again.

"Morgy!" yelled Byron. I turned around.

"Cool!" I said.

"Whoa!" said Haig, Billy, and Ferguson. The swing-set legs were sticking up straight, wobbling like giant spider legs. Then, as if the spider had decided to roll over, the legs swung gracefully down to the ground. Parents swarmed around, pushing, like ants around its ankles. Up went the crossbar, and there it stood. Dad climbed a ladder to check if it was level. Mr. Noonan put stones under a low leg. Mom checked a clipboard.

"OK, now, who's going to Home Depot for the cement? Laura Noonan has money for you," she was saying when a cement mixer drove up.

A big guy with red hair got out. "Now, I can put it in a wheelbarrow or directly in the holes," he said.

"Oh. Laura?" said Mom. "I don't think we ordered this. We might have called you for a price, but we can't afford it."

"Are you the lady that worked with my Rudy? With the knittin'?" asked the man.

"Yes," said Mom.

He took her hand in both of his. "It's left over from

a job. With my compliments," he said. Ferguson got to pull the lever to release the cement. The cement flowed, the parents smoothed, and it was done.

Dad put up sawhorses, and Byron and I ran around and around the swing set with caution tape. It started raining, so we got in our cars.

Mom and Byron's mom stayed out a few more minutes on the hill behind the swings, talking. Then they hugged and ran down to the cars. Mom got in.

"What were you talking about?" said Dad.

"About next year," said Mom. "The slide."

That week, Mr. Noonan put mulch underneath and hung up eight swings, and there was another thing to do at recess. If you swung really high, you could see one window of our house, behind a tree.

One day Mrs. Caitland said, "Today is our day to beautify our new playground. Mrs. Noonan and Miss Merriweather from the Garden Club have flowers. Anyone who wants to plant may take a pot and do so. But please follow their instructions."

Aunt Mary and the lady with the blue knit hat were standing under the tree, saying, "Marigolds or petunias?" to the kids as they came along.

I chose marigolds. "Use the holes we dug," said Miss Merriweather, "and place them firmly. Just a little dirt over the top," she told everyone.

Aunt Mary winked at me. "Any day now, dear." She was talking about Mom having the twins. It was still cold out. My marigolds jiggled in the wind. I thought it would be warm by the time the twins came.

They came that night. Dad and Mom dropped me off at the Noonans' on their way to the hospital. The next morning I wondered why I was waking up on the Noonans' couch with Aunt Mary sitting on the arm. She was knitting something little and pink. "Phoebe and Penelope," she said.

Phoebe and Penelope? How do they think up these names? I wondered, and closed my eyes again. When I opened them, Aunt Mary was still there.

"If you'd like to skip school and visit them, I wouldn't say no," she said. So we went to the hospital.

They were in little plastic boxes in the nursery with all the other babies. It took a while to figure out which ones they were. They had hats on. Their faces were wrinkled and red like two thumbs with open mouths.

"Healthy lungs," said Aunt Mary. We went to the cafeteria and got Mom a milkshake.

"How do you feel?" I said.

"Lighter, much lighter," said Mom, and she slurped with her straw.

Mom and the twins came home that week, just

when it got warm outside. Savanna was coming to help at the end of the school year. Dad got time off from work. It was messy and screamy at our house. The babies' legs were little and red. They kicked them when they cried. They looked just like little bee legs.

Pancake would try to get in Mom's lap when she nursed them. Mom would look at me, and I'd pick him up so that he wouldn't feel left out. So there would be Mom nursing one twin, Dad giving the other one a bottle, and me with Pancake. He liked me to rub the stripes on his forehead with my knuckles. I put my face in his fur and said, "What are we going to do with all these babies?" so no one would hear. He batted my ears.

One afternoon when I got home, Dad went to Mack's to get some formula and the paper. Mom was nursing Penelope. "Rraw, rrraw," yelled Phoebe. I went in the babies' room. Her leg was kicking, and her little chin was shaking. "Rraw, rraw, gasp, rraw." I reached under her and picked her up. She weighed about as much as Pancake, but she was harder. "Rrraw, rrraw." It was like being in a storm. I nestled her in my arm. I made sure her head didn't flop. She roared. I walked around.

I got to the window that looks out on the old dead-looking maple tree. Only it wasn't dead. It had little, wrinkled, baby green leaves on it. I could see the park. The chipper truck had cleaned up the branches that blew down over the winter. The grass looked like a tucked-in blanket. The girl with long black hair and her grandmother were walking to the baseball diamond with the other grandchildren. Three had on uniforms. Miss Merriweather was buying the crossing guard an ice cream from the Good Humor truck. Off on the hill, the swing set glinted. It all looked so nice and peaceful.

Then I noticed it was nice and peaceful inside, too. Phoebe was looking up at a spiderweb.

I could feel her little heart beating against my arm. She felt softer. She looked down from the spiderweb to me. Her eyes were big and blue and so new that the whites were blue, too. She kept looking, as if she were trying to figure something out.

"I'm your big brother," I said. She looked and looked. "It's going to be great. You have a weird name, but you were born here, so it's OK. And if there's anything you don't know, you can ask me. I know all about this place."

Or I will, by the time they can talk.